BARE
BEAR

Jez Alborough

HODDER AND STOUGHTON
SYDNEY AUCKLAND LONDON TORONTO

First published by Ernest Benn Limited, England.
This edition first published 1986 by
Hodder & Stoughton (Australia) Pty Ltd
2 Apollo Place, Lane Cove, NSW, 2066.

National Library of Australia Cataloguing-in-Publication entry
Alborough, Jez
Bare Bear
ISBN 0 340 37446 2
1. Children's stories. English
I. Title.
823'.914
Printed by Tien Wah Press Singapore

for Jenny

To keep warm in
the arctic air,

a polar bear wears
polar wear.

On his back a polar suit

and on his foot . . .

a polar boot.

His gloves are really

quite fantastic,

attached to him
by pink elastic.

His socks he changes
once a week:

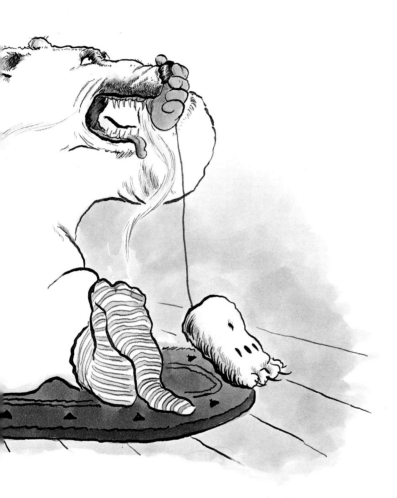

no wonder all his tootsies reek!

Can you credit

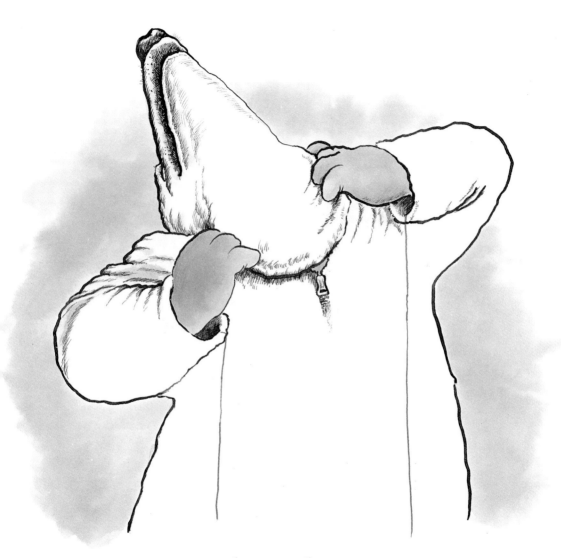

such palaver

to pull away a balaclava?

He zips his zip
and under there . . .

pale blue polar underwear.

He mutters: 'Keep your
peepers shut',

and I know you would do
but . . .

in bare bear books
expect to find . . .

a great big, bulging
bear behind.